There is a mirror in the pocket. Remove the film on it and
USE IT to
EXPLORE and
CHANGE

The pictures
in this
book

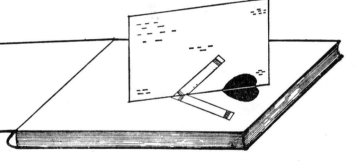

ANNETTE

Devised by
MARION WALTER

Illustrated by
NAVAH HABER-SCHAIM

 André Deutsch

By the same author
MAKE A BIGGER PUDDLE MAKE A SMALLER WORM

First published 1971 by
André Deutsch Limited
105 Great Russell Street London WC1

Printed in Great Britain by
Morrison and Gibb Ltd., Edinburgh

ISBN 0 233 96339 1

To my niece Annette

who likes to pick daisies

Can you see Annette ?

Hello Annette

Sometimes Annette is happy

But sometimes she is sad

Make her look happy

Don't make her look sad !

Annette has one ribbon

in her hair

Can you put the other there ?

What else can you do ?

On her foot she has one shoe

Put the other one on too.

Her pet looks funny

Is it her cat

or is it her bunny?

Can you see

all of her red ball?

What else can you change?

Annette has a bear

Put all of him there

Here is her bear.

What can you do

So that she has two ?

She would like to have more

Can she have three—or four ?

Annette likes to watch birds

hop and fly.

Now you make some more

hop by.

She likes to pick daisies

Can you see many ?

Or hardly any ?

She likes to hang clothes

on the line.

Can you help her ?

Now you have met Annette

Good bye Annette

If you have enjoyed this book, you will also enjoy *Make a Bigger Puddle, Make a Smaller Worm*, another Mirror Book by Marion Walter.